W9-CFJ-681

OTHER BOOKS FROM KANE/MILLER

One Woolly Wombat

The Magic Bubble Trip

The House From Morning to Night

Wilfrid Gordon McDonald Partridge

The Park Bench

I Want My Potty

Girl From the Snow Country

Cat In Search of a Friend

The Truffle Hunter

Goodbye Rune

The Umbrella Thief

First American Paperback Edition, 1988

First American Edition 1986 by Kane/Miller Book Publishers
Brooklyn, New York & La Jolla, California

Originally published in Spain in 1981 under the title
Cepillo by Ediciones Hymsa, Barcelona, Spain
Copyright © Pere Calders and Carme Solé Vendrell 1981
American text copyright © Kane/Miller Book Publishers 1986
All rights reserved. For information contact:
Kane/Miller Book Publishers
P.O. Box 529, Brooklyn, New York 11231

Library of Congress Cataloging-in-Publication Data

Calders, Pere, 1912–
  Brush.

  Translation of: Cepillo.
  Summary: When a little boy adopts a large brush to
replace his banished dog, the brush surprises him by
coming to life and actually behaving like a dog.
  [1. Brooms and brushes—Fiction. 2. Dogs—Fiction]
I. Solé Vendrell, Carme, 1944–   , ill. II. Title.
PZ7.C12714Br 1986   [E]   85-23873
ISBN 0-916291-05-7
ISBN 0-916291-16-2 (pbk.)

Printed and bound in Tokyo by Dai Nippon Printing Company
2 3 4 5 6 7 8 9 10

BRUSH

By PERE CALDERS

Illustrated by CARME SOLÉ VENDRELL

Translated by Marguerite Feitlowitz

A CRANKY NELL BOOK

KM Kane/Miller Book Publishers

Brooklyn, New York & La Jolla, California

The day that Turco—a little pistol of a pup—ate Señor Sala's hat, Señora Sala decided that enough was enough and that it would take the patience of a saint to put up with this mischief any longer.

So she got the whole family together and asked each member his opinion of the situation. It was decided that the gardener's married daughter would take Turco and keep him in her house.

Little Sala was so sad he thought he'd die. To him it seemed there was no way to go on living without his little pup.

After he stopped crying, however, he realized he had to fill the emptiness left by Turco's absence. First he tried to imagine his aunt's canary as a companion, but the number of really fun things he could do with the bird were so few, he immediately knew they could never be close friends.

Then he imagined that the floor lamp in the library was a faithful soldier. For nearly two hours he thought he had solved his problem, but soon it was clear that he still longed for his beloved Turco.

He tried to create a lasting friendship with a canvas ball, with a ball of string, with an American-made top, with a new flower in the garden and then with a long cane which had been the envy of all his friends. But he discovered that however brave he tried to be, he could not overcome his loneliness, and that the difference between all those things and a dog was so great that it was impossible to forget Turco.

He knew that what he needed was to find a substitute for him, something that could take the dog's place yet not destroy his memory.

He went through the house from top to bottom, turning the closets and drawers inside out and finally, in a corner of the attic, he found a very big brush, one that was no longer in style and had been banished forever from the family broom closet.

He closed his eyes and passed his hand over its bristles. He had the definite impression he was petting a dog. In fact, this first encounter felt so good that Little Sala decided not to search any further.

He tied the brush to some string and in less than five minutes was no longer even aware he was dragging a brush behind him. Rather he believed Brush was a dog of rare pedigree who was following him all over the house.

By evening, Little Sala was tired from trailing his new friend around and went to lie down.

Before getting into bed, he tied Brush to a chair. But no sooner had he tied it up when he was overcome by a wave of tenderness. He couldn't help thinking of how tame and gentle Brush was and how willing it was to play all sorts of games.

The idea that Brush would spend the night tied up sleeping on the cold floor made him feel bad. So he jumped down, untied Brush and took it into bed with him.

Soon Little Sala noticed that the brush was warm and was snuggling up against him for a hug. This, naturally, was very serious, because it's one thing to pretend to change a brush into a dog, but it's another thing if the change really happens.

Little Sala got up, turned on the light and was astonished to see that the brush, though it still looked exactly like a brush, was moving around like a dog.

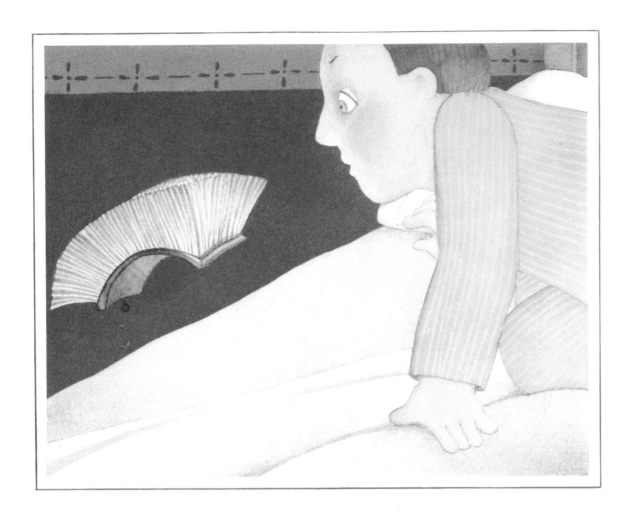

It turned a few somersaults and then showed its stomach to be scratched.

Anyone watching this would have wondered how a brush that still looked like a brush could have paws to move about on and a stomach to scratch. But once the problem of giving life to the brush had been solved, such details didn't matter and weren't worth worrying about.

That's what Little Sala thought, and right away he wanted to tell his parents about the marvelous event. But he knew better than to wake his parents in the middle of the night and decided to wait until the next morning.

Of course, he couldn't sleep all night and, very early, as soon as he heard his mother up and about, he went downstairs with Brush under his arms.

"Look, Mama," he said. "I found a brush that is really a dog. It moves, knows my voice and has fleas."

Without interrupting her chores, his mother looked at him and said, ''Don't be silly and get rid of that piece of junk. You're old enough to be a little more sensible.''

He was hurt and thought again about how grown-ups acted like they knew it all yet did many foolish things themselves.

He said nothing more, brought Brush to his room and thought that if they didn't want to believe him, it didn't matter. They'd be the losers.

At dinner, his mother jokingly told about Little Sala's discovery, and his father laughed as though it were the craziest thing in the world.

Little Sala didn't say anything, because he knew that ultimately justice prevails. Sooner or later, he knew, his family would realize that some things aren't what they seem and shouldn't be laughed at.

The next night he was awakened by Brush's howling. He heard the sounds of a struggle coming from the library and his father calling for help. Brush, looking strangely worried, poked at the door.

Little Sala opened the door, tiptoed down the stairs and saw his father fighting with a burglar who was stronger than he was and who was about to hit him on the head with a fire iron.

"Get him, Brush. Bite him!" he cried.

Brush ran like the wind and hurled himself at the burglar and bit him on the leg. The burglar was so surprised by the ferociousness of such a *thing*, that he immediately gave up and was handed over to the police, tied hand and foot.

A little later, his mother, with tears in her eyes, promised she would never again doubt her son's word, and his father, passing his hand over Brush's bristles, said, "We'll make a house for you in the garden, with all the latest conveniences. And above the door, we'll have painted:

WE'RE NOT SURE THAT IT'S ALIVE
BUT IT DESERVES TO BE!